The Great Swimming Race

Written by
Ann Bryant

Illustrated by
Peter Kavanagh

W
FRANKLIN WATTS
LONDON•SYDNEY

Ann Bryant

"I love swimming but I'm glad I'm not a fish because I think you can have too much of a good thing!"

Peter Kavanagh

"I live in Norfolk beside the sea. I love drawing and swimming, but I can't do both at the same time – the paper goes all soggy!"

Here at the sea side,

all ready to race,

5

Are Bonzo the Lobster

and Patti the Plaice,

7

Lulu the Octopus, Crusty the Crab,

Joshua Jet Fish and Dillon the Dab.

Crusty says: "Dillon
can't possibly win.
Look at him! Weedy
and thin as a pin!"

"I'll be the winner!" boasts
Joshua Jet.

"Forty-four races and not
beaten yet!"

"READY, SET, GO!"

The whistle is blown.

14

But Joshua thinks it's
his mobile ringtone.

The others dive in
with a flip and a flop.

And Joshua shouts,

"That's not fair! Make them stop!"

Referee Rocky says,

"Sorry, old mate.

They weren't too early.

You were too late!

"Also," he adds,
"mobile phones on the side
are breaking the rules.
You're DISQUALIFIED!"

Back in the water ...

"Watch out! There's a net!"

"You'll have to go round it!"

yells Joshua Jet.

So round they all swim,

led by Crusty the Crab,

Except for young Dillon,
that thin little Dab.

He wriggles his way

through a hole in the twine.

And swims for his life ...

25

... to the finishing line!

"Young Dillon's the winner!"
cries Rocky. "Well done!"

And Darren Dab grins at his
brother. "You WON!"

30

Notes for parents and teachers

READING CORNER has been structured to provide maximum support for new readers. The stories may be used by adults for sharing with young children. Primarily, however, the stories are designed for newly independent readers, whether they are reading these books in bed at night, or in the reading corner at school or in the library.

Starting to read alone can be a daunting prospect. READING CORNER helps by providing visual support and repeating words and phrases, while making reading enjoyable. These books will develop confidence in the new reader, and encourage a love of reading that will last a lifetime!

If you are reading this book with a child, here are a few tips:

1. Make reading fun! Choose a time to read when you and the child are relaxed and have time to share the story.

2. Encourage children to reread the story, and to retell the story in their own words, using the illustrations to remind them what has happened.

3. Give praise! Remember that small mistakes need not always be corrected.

READING CORNER covers three grades of early reading ability, with three levels at each grade. Each level has a certain number of words per story, indicated by the number of bars on the spine of the book, to allow you to choose the right book for a young reader:

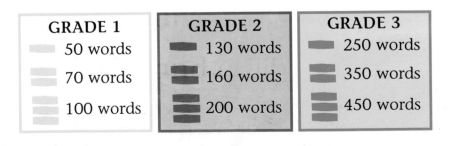

GRADE 1	GRADE 2	GRADE 3
50 words	130 words	250 words
70 words	160 words	350 words
100 words	200 words	450 words